Caught In-Between

Stefan Asemota

www.stefanasemota.com

© 2015
All rights reserved. No part of this publication may be reproduced, stored in a retrieval system or transmitted in any form by any means, electronic, mechanical, photocopying or otherwise, without first obtaining the written permission of the copyright owner

© Cover Painting
"El viaje en lo profundo"
Acryl sur toile 95 x 120
Malabo 2001
Simon Moncong
Farafinart.com

PREFACE

For perhaps the first time, we get a front-row viewing of what it feels like to be caught in between fatherhood and divorce; being culturally rudderless and constantly subjected to cultural segregation; love and letting go: acceptance and denial, and everything in between.

DEDICATION

This book is for
My dad who taught me manliness,
My mother who taught me femininity,
Femi who taught me Sight,
Seyi who thought me Life,
Jasmin who taught me to believe,
Barbara who taught me be,
Thomas who taught me structure,
Teddy who taught me manhood,
Nathalie who sent me to the school of hard knocks,
Zvezdin who taught me laughter…

Many thanks to
Christine,
Camilo,
Family Omo,
My In-laws (Old and New),
Family and close friends

Introduction

The analysis of the causes behind my divorce and stagnation of my career caught in-between the determination to move forward as a father and partner, prompted me to take time off work to rethink a few things.

At 38.7, I am resetting my life. I have quit my job at SOFTCOM. I have quit my studio in Berne. I am now about to leave Switzerland for an undefined period of time to resolve my puzzles, pursue my new goals and sort-out my in-betweens, somewhere else. The place? I don't know yet. But knowing what to do is more important than where to do it.

I am excited about this looming experience and look forward to sharing these moments with Femi, Seyi and Jasmin.

If by chance I shall be unable to solve my puzzles, I shall take some drastic measures or do some crazy stuff. Put no actions past me, for I am a desperate man struggling to free myself from this hellish purgatory of in-betweens.

Contents

Two Side	15
Caught in-between	18
The journey	24
Singing Priest	29
Bank X	33
Vagabonds in Power (V.I.P)	38
Las Gidi	43
Break or bake a cookie	48
Middle Class	58
Food	62
Driver's Licence	65
ATM's and Network issues	69
CMS	71
Onikan	75
Bank Y	77
After work	81
God is Good	86
Benin, a decaying City	90
Wudu	97
How it all goes down	**100**

Foreword

"It requires a good amount of humility, sobriety, and courage to live in a cultural confluence - of confusion - and of identity crises."

Identity crisis. Everyone wears it like a badge - but then it's up to you to label this badge however you want. This badge could be a source of shame, insecurity, pressure, and even suicidal instincts. To wear this badge publicly is not only bold, but extremely butt-pinching crazy. We've all battled some mild form of identity crisis and never felt the need to share, but now, I realize we've been selfish. We've been timid. We've been scared. So, we bury the tails of our monumental insecurities in between our fearful legs. Hoping that no one perceives the stench of our rotting soul. We suffer alone.

I've always imagined what people's reaction would be if they could read a transcript of our minds, especially the chapters that chronicle every aspect of our struggles. I would imagine that it would be a scary thought for everyone to have the contents of their diary on full display for the world. Honestly, this is one reason why most people never kept a diary. There's this primal need to guard ones primitive thoughts from the intrusion of unfriendly eyes and judgmental tongues.
Caught In-Between captures the existential insecurities of a young man, battling the

complex ironies of being raised with a broken cultural compass. Yet in this darkly woven prose, the poetic confluence of humor and pain characterize the putrid instincts of humanity, and humanity's quick-wittedness in casting macabre judgment based purely on how odd the shade of ones skin is.

We're perhaps all guilty of treating people who are different from us a little bit differently - maybe differently in a good way, or differently in a not-so-good way. But we oftentimes notice and acknowledge this difference in the way we interact and deal with them. Our reactions to this difference may be subconscious, in that we don't go out of our way to analyze and direct our reactions to this perceived difference.

Lagos (a Nigerian city, at the center of the author's journey) as a city of parallels suffers from its own fair share of identity crises. A city comprised of several cultural boroughs. There's a Lagos for the rich and a Lagos for the poor, but even in the complexity of the math, we've always found a common ground for cohabitation.

In recent times, as self-proclaimed leader of the Free World, the United States has made attempts at dousing race tensions by electing the first ever black president of the United States of America, but whatever score Barack Obama's exalted office has garnered for the black race is quickly dissipated by a much bigger, systemic, and subconscious cultural segregation of a growing population of mulattoes.

For perhaps the first time, we get a front-row viewing of what it feels like to be caught in between fatherhood and divorce; being culturally rudderless and constantly subjected to cultural segregation; love and letting go: acceptance and denial, and everything in between.

In a brutally honest narrative, the author takes us on a mentally stimulating cultural journey with all the trappings and magic of a travelogue, penned with unintended mystery and suspense, encapsulated in self-flagellating humor.

James Amuta
Author, Enigma: Beyond the Poet

Two Side

Diversity and complexity live in me – they have taken residence within me – and they cast an ominous shadow over me on a daily basis. I come from a long line of "caught in-betweens". There is no root to my matter. I am multi-rooted – my cultural axis is like the two opposite sides of a magnet, Side Y being Swiss and Side X being Nigerian (order is irrelevant).

Side Y: Switzerland is more or less just about chocolates, Cuckoo clocks and banks. Switzerland is geographically and culturally sublime! Switzerland is that perfect postcard you buy in any kiosk round the world. But even there you find "stupid human beings" that grounded Swissair and messed up the great banks!

Luckily they have Roger Federer to help them make up for their misdeeds and mischiefs.

Today, Switzerland is caught in-between the European community, neutrality and in-neutrality, banks and bank secrecy.

Side X: Nigeria on its own is a big caught in-between. It is a pulsating powerhouse that is the most populous nation on the African continent, about to EXPLODE!

History tells us that Nigeria was a peaceful country until 1472. Suddenly it was visited by an idiotic Portuguese, who had nothing better doing than jumping on his boat and sailing down south with a great idea of introducing Roman Catholicism into Nigeria. Don't get me wrong. I love the Portuguese; one of my very good friends Paulo from Fribourg is Portuguese.

Thereafter, a Briton, Sir George Dashwood Taubman Goldie sailed in to claim Nigeria; he brought along western corruptions and journalism. As if all this was not enough, Flora Shaw later coined the name "Nigeria" from our own river Niger! A Brit, giving us our country name! What a shame. Maybe that's the main reason why most of our Nigerian girls play with white Barbie dolls which resulted in a large percentage of Nigerian girls spending half of their monthly budget on wigs (imported from brazil and wherever else they can find similar quality) thinking a real woman MUST have long silky hair. LMAO.

Don't get me wrong here again! I love the Brits - one of my most important childhood friends, Oscar is also British!

The problem neither being Portuguese nor British. The problem is some "stupid human being" making decisions and manipulating his entourage. Human beings are so complex because of the property of emergence. They think they can just come in, change and take everything.

Nigeria has no super achiever to me, except Wole Soyinka, Ken Saro-Wiva, Dele Giwa, Fela Kuti, and the late great Oba Ovonramwen of the Benin kingdom. These are the only people I know who are not "caught in-between". I think I was born hundred years too late, I would have preferred being born during the period of Oba Ovonramwen the Great. I would have fought under him. If the great Oba of Benin left it to me, I would have organized thousands of Benin soldiers, armed them with cutlasses, taken them to the coastal front to watch over Nigeria. If any invaders came in, we would have slit their throats like a bulb of orange, just as they stepped foot on Nigerian soil!

Today, Nigeria is caught in-between identity and modernity, continuity and change, Christianity and ancient Nigerian religion, corruption and prosperity, the wealthy and Vagabonds in Power.

Caught in-between

At a much younger age, I usually responded aggressively to questions concerning my ethnicity. I had difficulties in understanding why people just couldn't let skin colour or cultural affiliation be. It went so far that I fought fellow classmates in school who racially insulted my parents or me.

The fact that I was a Benin boy and hardly spoke the Benin language exempted me from important family discussions and gatherings. My dad was never willing to teach me and never understood why it was important for me to learn his mother tongue.

My uncles and aunties always challenged me over my inability to speak my mother tongue. To them, this was a cancerous sign of weakness. It was more important for my father that I became a doctor or took over his business than for me to learn a simple language. Even today, I sometimes get insulted for not speaking my native language despite the fact that I tried my very best at grabbing little bits from day to day conversations.

Well this language issue is actually something very common with children growing up in a multilingual environment. 60% of my secondary school friends / classmates can't speak their native language.

My societal acceptance over the years evolved rapidly both in linguistics and integration. I am now able to look at the various ways which my mixed-heritage has influenced the quality of my life. I have had various struggles surrounding my identity and resilience. With time, I asserted the need for continued vigilance in discerning how society's "race rules" could cause extra stress.

I would like to highlight some of these mind-states I experienced over the years:

- **Confused** when someone says: they want to marry within their race.
- **Frustrated** when someone asks me: what are you?
- **Irritated** when people assume, I am just one thing or another!
- So **happy** when I realize the rich history that led to my existence.
- **Anticipation**, for getting to share different cultures.
- **Stunned**, when I am out with my mum and someone asks if I was adopted?
- **Joy**, when I get to talk about just my culture and myself.
- **Annoyance**, when a job application asks me to "select only one ethnicity".
- **Happiness**, when I look at my sons.

I personally feel mixed people are "life's gifts" to a "better world". I see mixed people as an updated version of two or more cultures railroaded together. We are the missing link; we are the bridge connecting two or more important points.
I believe we are here to convey a "message" to the world. Instead of our message to be heard we find ourselves constantly placed in-between our dual roots.

I get confronted with issues and situations related to my ethnic differences more in Nigeria than Switzerland. My last experience in Nigeria was quite daunting. It happened at the Passport and immigration office in Benin City two years ago. I had intentions of renewing my Nigerian passport. I dully completed the necessary forms and submitted them to the customs officer, whom I shall refer to as Officer Q. Officer Q kept me waiting for no reason while other people that arrived after me were already being handed out other forms to fill. After sitting down patiently for an hour (like a typical Swiss), I decided, it was time to activate my "first Nigerian side". I stood up, walked towards Officer Q and asked him in plain English; "Sir, I have being waiting for an hour now, is there any problem with my application?" Officer Q fixed his eyes on me and said:
Officer Q: Oga, I will need a judicial attestation, which certifies that you are a Nigerian!

I replied: You're joking? Who is asking for this?
Officer Q: I'm not joking.
I asked: so tell me, how does a certified Nigerian look like?
Officer Q: Oga, calm down or else I go suspend your application.
I, totally raging with inner anger, felt it was high time I brought out my "second Nigerian side". So I asked him in Pidgin English (the tone of my Benin style pidgin sounds so local. Only people that were born and bred in Benin can speak like this.), "Oga mi, forget my application! In fact give me my application make I tear am myself!"
Officer Q took a couple of steps back and just starred at me.
I continued: Oga, I ask you question before; how person weh be Nigerian wan resemble? I no dey comot for here until you reply me o.
Everyone in the waiting room started applauding and supporting me. Some were even shouting at Officer Q. The atmosphere really got tense, so tense that we started exchanging "unnecessary words". I was very angry, I actually felt like punching him straight to the face. Suddenly to my surprise a higher-ranking officer came in between us. The higher-ranking officer directed me to his office. As I walked in, he apologized for the reaction of the junior Officer Q. The senior officer collected my forms, reviewed them and vetoed on them. Within half an hour, I had my passport photo and thumbprint taken and my signature scanned. 45 minutes later, I was handed out my passport 'collect slip'.

On my way out, I came across Officer Q. I asked him, "Oga, I no dey joke oh, you never answer my question." He seemed still dumbfounded and transfused. I then added. "Shay na 5pm you dey close, I go dey wait for you outside." Then I left.

Not too long afterwards, the heavens signalled that it would soon spill its contents. I had to hasten to my car, parked within the premises of the Passport Office. At the gate, I observed the same young officer Q at the gate "harassing" fellow officers of the opposite sex. He and the "games" he was making advances at are likely co-habitants of the passport office I had just left. I got a useful lesson, whatever the circumstances; life just has to go on. And in Nigeria, as we say, you must shine your eyes – open them wide and scream if you wish to get your voice heard. There's very little room for gentlemen in this country.

Back to my other matter, I have been living in "caught in-betweens" for as long as I can remember. Having a "biracial Identity" is a forced choice dilemma, which I will have to live with all my life.

My caught in-betweens could fill the Eifel Tower with books to read for a decade but I would rather only highlight seven (7):
   1. Caught in-between Stefan and Stephan
   2. Caught in-between Black and White

3. Caught in-between ethnic values and fatherhood
4. Caught in-between three languages partly perfectly spoken
5. Caught in-between Benin boy and unable to speak Edo
6. Caught in-between failure and desire
7. Caught in-between Nigeria and Switzerland

In Switzerland I am boxed into different yet colourful stereotypes; I could be seen as a foreigner, a Nigerian, a drug dealer, a top footballer, a hip-hop singer or a Swiss-Nigerian but hardly a Swiss. This does not imply that the Swiss are racist but rather 'classist'.

In Nigeria I am also boxed, paraded, and sold on different shelves; I could be Oyibo (white), Yellow (white), a Bank (Rich), an Hausa elite, an Arab, a Swiss but hardly a Nigerian. This does not imply that Nigerians are racist but rather victims of an imperial class system imposed on them by their former colonial masters.

The journey

Destination Lagos. There are various ways of flying to Lagos from Switzerland. I chose the transit via Pariser Charles de Gaulle airport (which is named after a French general). My journey started from Basel Muhlhouse Airport in Switzerland with a charter Jet.

Charles de Gaulle is a massive airport. It took me 34 minutes to reach my final departing Gate. After I got to my gate, I rushed for a quick fresh coffee before boarding the Airbus. Boarded the plane, found my seat and made myself confortable. The pilot called for the cabin doors to be armed by the cabin crew. We were set to take-off!

Once we reached our cruising altitude, an Air France crewmember handed out a health questionnaire to be filled by in-coming tourists. I said to me self: "ooh I seem to have forgotten about 'that issue' the 'past Ebola' situation in Lagos."

For lunch I had Gratin de Légumes à La Vache qui Rit served. My subconscious simply did not share my laudable intentions. I just couldn't stop thinking about Ebola and the Boko Haram issues. A sudden tossing in the plane brought me back to a state of consciousness. I suddenly enjoyed looking out the oval window over the mystic Sahara dessert. I have always been intrigued by the Sahara and it remains undoubtedly a place I must visit! I hope I can make the journey once with Fadele, my other good friend, who has, mind you, adventured the London- Lagos journey by car (Peugeot 505 GTI) and bike, three times.

The Air France crew embarked on their last drink trolley service before arrival. I ordered my last cup of coffee in French. The crewmember looked at me with great surprise. She said, "You speak faultless French! You don't look French." I said, "There I go again; how does a French look? White? Who gives a fuck how a French looks!! I am willing to take the coffee and your first comment but keep the other fucking comment! I don't need this." She looked at me, shocked. In hindsight, I may have been a little hard on the crewmember, but in my defence, the world has been harsh to me all my life.

At the same time another crewmember was busy arguing with a passenger. The passenger wanted his 8th bottle of wine but the crewmember did not give it to him. I felt the crewmember acted correctly and professionally. What a job!

You actually know when the plane has touched down on Lagos soil if you see most Nigerians unlocking their seat belts, standing up and retrieving their bags from the overhead luggage compartment whilst the seat belt lights are

STILL turned on! The sight of this was certainly not funny for the cabin crewmembers.

All in all the French cabin crew where fabulous and very professional, we had good weather and a vibrant Nigerian/French atmosphere.

I giggle uncontrollably when plane doors are opened on arrival at any airport (especially on Nigerian in-bound flights). I love the feeling of the heat flowing in, the atmosphere around the plane, the noise and the people. It's fabulous! I can still trace these feelings back to the trips I made as a child with my mum.

After landing, the same crewmember came to me and apologised, she told me she understood why I was annoyed. I in turn also apologised to her, told her I was sorry the way I reacted. We departed from each other, smiling.

After disembarking from the Airbus, I was welcomed by a young Nigerian health student, who handed me an Ebola pamphlet. Walking further, I was received by a health officer to whom I handed out my Health questionnaire duly filled. In return she took a picture of me and also pasted an Ebola Alert sticker on the back of my Nigerian passport. This sticker contained various information and health guidelines. What really stirred my mind was the twenty-one day symptom period printed in Red with a bold font. It stated that: if a traveller identifies any of the mentioned symptoms within the first twenty-one days, he should call the hotline number printed at the bottom of the sticker!

Baggage Claim and Customs were done in less than an hour! I was so surprised but yet impressed. I can definitely recall spending more time with customs, arguing about unimportant things. The most significant arguments I ever had with Nigerian Customs were about my passport validity. Nigeria remains the only country I know, that makes it difficult for their citizens to travel into. Apparently those times have changed! Now I am officially in Lagos, happy to be back!

Coming out of the arrival hall, feeling the 35 degrees Celsius (+ humidity) and seeing Chinedu, is always a deep pleasure. Divine happiness. I've known Chinedu since I was 5 years old, and we have been best friends ever since. With Chinedu I have played, cried; created a little football team; I have celebrated and feasted with him a bunch of times. I was happy to see that we haven't changed a bit over all these years despite distance and time.

Chinedu and I made our way through the arrival crowd, to the car park, where we drove off into Lagos. We stopped by at one of Chinedu's favourite spots "La Mango". La Mango is a bar, lounge, and restaurant erected in a calm, "secured" area somewhere in Ikeja. I say secured mainly because Lagos Nights can get quite sketchy at times. La Mango has a nice swimming pool surrounded with Palms. Whilst there I had the chance of ordering my first "goat-meat" pepper soup! I have always been a fan of pepper soup since childhood. Pepper-soup is a broth-like spicy, tasty bouillon soup usually served hot with a locally brewed cold beer preferably Star.

After our short break at La Mango, we now made our way to Chinedu's home.

But all in all, I am happy to spend the next few weeks in Lagos. Lagos is a gateway to everything! And Lagosians are interesting, outspoken, loud, authentic Nigerians and I am happy to see that Lagos hasn't lost its panache despite the recent Ebola scare. In fact I can promise you, I haven't thought about Ebola during my first hours in Lagos! And I doubt if it shall come to my mind over the next few weeks.

Singing Priest

It's 6.00 am, this fine Saturday morning and I was thrown out of my bed by a singing street pastor with a microphone! He was singing praises of God and chanting with a lady. I couldn't see the looks of him, but from his voice I could tell he was someone joyful, someone with enormous positivity.

But come to think about it, nothing short of incense seems to raise the hairs on your back than chanting. Back in primary school we also chanted a lot in the mornings before stepping into class. Chanting was used to teach the children through repetition. But this kind of chanting was different. I tend to believe that the singing pastor might be looking to expand his congregation. To me, it was just another new church opening up (maybe). There are more churches in Nigeria than any other nation on earth. But the credibility of most of them is in doubt, because the more one looks at the congregation, the less Christianity one sees in their lives outside the walls of their churches.

Money. It is said is the root of all evils, and it is the only reason the current trend in the Christian community has been drawing many pastors farther from God every single day. There was a time when Christian missionaries were renowned for their simple lifestyle. Jesus Christ himself had no shoes, only sandals. These same missionaries would leave the comfort of their homes, to live in other African countries. They endured the hardship the natives suffered in a bid to impart in them the knowledge of Jesus Christ as well as transfer meaningful education that would improve their lives. The early pastors (or more aptly, missionaries) were always there for their congregation, tending to their needs and this was passed across to their successors who were Africans, but the legacy of the likes of Reverend Ajayi Crowther who spent their entire lives ministering to the spiritual needs of members and widening the knowledge scope of Nigerians generally has since dissipated to a more self-centred doctrine.

I believe that Christianity, and churches as we see them today in Nigeria are bereft of the TRUE success story. Let me give a brief synopsis on the book of my Christian life, before I explain. I am a Christian; I believe in a Supreme Being called God; in our Lord and saviour Jesus Christ and the Holy Spirit.

Baptised, I grew up in a classic Christian Nigerian family, classic in the sense that we said prayers once in a while before eating (both at home and in school). I attended church services on a regular basis (NOT just every Sunday at 9am). My grand father was also a born Christian.

After over 170 years of Christianity in Nigeria, Nigerian Christians have not been able to unite Christianity and Nigeria's indigenous religions. Lets be frank here, Christianity from its earliest history has maintained a negative attitude towards other religious traditions as practised by people on the African and Asian continents.

In order for Christianity to be well integrated in Nigeria, there must be a genuine dialogue with existing Nigerian indigenous religions that existed long before the Europeans arrived our shores.

My father thought me that God never named the church because you never need to name anything there is only one of! From my biblical understanding the word church ALWAYS referenced either the body of Christ or the body of God.

It seems to me that Christianity in Africa has not adequately tapped resources that can make Christianity authentically African.

Church business is certainly big business with several pastors now boasting of private jets, some even own more than one jet. I stumbled across a write-up, which listed the ten richest Nigerian pastors. All of the listed idiotic pastors had a minimum of two private jets. The so-called pastor that shocked me the most was Bishop David Oyedepo who had a fully-fledged 35 million-dollar Gulfstream Jet!

Breff, back to my singing priest, I hope he won't be waking me up every morning!

Bank X

Another day is dawn and on my bucket list of items stood some bureaucratic errands. I planned on opening a savings account at one of the oldest banks in Nigeria, Bank X, the Ikeja Branch. I also planned on renewing my driver's licence, going to the couturiere to sew some new cloths, taking a footprint to make some sandals at the cobbler's.

I had no appointment at the Bank, but I wanted to be in early. I had to take along eight passport photos (of which just four were used), a photocopy of an electric bill and a valid passport. After I gathered all these documents together, I made my way to the Bank where I was asked by security to open my rucksack; it was scanned for unwanted items (such as guns, etc.). After entering the building, I made my way upstairs. There was a security man standing and directing people to various niches. I told him, I would like to open an account. He directed me to the last room down the hall to my right. Got to the room, found out there were 6 people seated and waiting.

I asked politely, "Opening of new accounts?" and a random guy replied "yes". I said "thanks". I walked in and took a seat.
I barely waited ten minutes before a man I presumed to be a bank clerk, in his late

twenties greeted me and told me to come with him. The other people gazed at me as if I was a goat about to be eaten up by a lion. For a second I was rooted in frustration, I found myself caught in-between again; should I stay or go? I presumed I was supposed to be last person to be called. I just did not understand why the bank clerk came for me. So I ignored his first call, then he insisted, by pointing and yelling, "I am talking to you! Come with me". As I stood up, I heard a random voice saying: "That's Nigeria for you, that's the way it works."

As I left the waiting room, I informed him, "I think it was not my turn yet, I just arrived." And he replied, "They can wait!"

The whole opening account process took me two hours, which I find personally reasonable. But I believe a "conventional" Nigerian without some sort of connections would take at least three hours.

The positive thing about my sojourn at the bank was receiving my ATM card - the same day.

My impressions of the Bank X atmosphere DOES NOT cover that of other Nigerian banks, but I must admit that things are slowly improving.

Once I left the bank, I engaged on my second rendezvous, which was with Chinedu's couturiere. I am such a big fan of Monsieur Sunday Balogun. Sunday is just one of those

Lagosians striving each and everyday. Sunday's shop is situated somewhere near Surulere. As I walked into Sunday's Shop (which is about 4 X 5 meter squared) I found him sitting behind his old German sewing machine all dressed up in a solid red bow-tie, white crisp short sleeve shirt, black pants with black suede shoes. Toujours chic Monsieur Balogun!

His sewing machine is centred in the middle of the room just under his ceiling fan. To the left of the sewing machine, stands an old wooden table, which serves as his worktable. To the right lie piles of traditional and western materials in rolls. Sunday has been in the couture business for over ten years. He took time off to speak with me and also showed me his latest modelling pictures taken the week before for a top modelling agency.

The only thing that drives me almost mad in Lagos is its Traffic jams. One can't get from point A to B without getting stuck in a silly "go slow" as the Lagosians call it! To give you an idea, shuttling between Surulere and Ikeja could cost you two hours or more on a very bad day whereas on a Good day, it may only be just thirty minutes. Problem is; there are hardly any good days!

I finally postponed my drivers licence registration because of traffic. At the end, I thought it would be easier if I just got it done in Benin City.

At times I find myself lamenting about NEPA (Nigerian Electric Power Authority) a lot. NEPA follows you anywhere you go. Light fluctuation in Lagos or Nigeria as a whole is still a big problem. The NEPA still runs on facilities that where installed by the British decades ago. NEPA's philosophy is having electricity during the day and use candles at night (vice-versa also works). Absence of electricity makes it very difficult to sustain meat, milk and complicates the pumping of water. Almost every Nigerian household has one or two generators that either run on petrol or diesel. I had more "generator powered" nights than "NEPA powered nights".

It is funny how people (a whole nation) have gotten used to things NOT working. And even when things do work people get scared. I have lived with this NEPA Issues since I was a child. It is sad to experience that in 2015 (after over 54 years of Nigerian independence), we Nigerians still have to spend sweat-soaked nights, illuminated by candles.

No light, no water leads to bad business and definitely bad health! Electricity should be a priority for the entire population, most especially the healthcare sector.

Nevertheless, I seem to be getting used to the dry, dust-bearing wind from the northeast. Sleep at night is getting much better since I adapted an old travel technique I acquired back in Thailand, which is sleeping on the floor.

Foam mattress generally absorbs body heat and radiates it back; while floor tiles convert your body heat.

Vagabonds in Power (V.I.P)

One day, on my way back from Chinedu's, I saw a billboard campaign ad for a candidate running for the presidential elections. The board said: "One free meal a day, in public schools!" At the same time I recall a proverb, which contradicts this particular campaign advert. The proverb goes: "No piss for my back tell me say rain dey fall".

The year I was born, Olusegun Obasanjo was made president. He was the first illiterate and vagabond I experienced in my early years of growing up. He had a Doctorate Degree in stealing over 200 billion dollars! Things did not get better with each and every election or coup thereafter.

After Olusegun Obasanjo, we had Shehu Shagari; I nicknamed him Puppet. During his civilian government, the political crime nexus reached its peak because the same military warlords that installed him controlled him and with his help, expanded their organized crime to other political sectors.

I must not forget the evil genius known as Ibrahim Babangida. A handful of fabulous Muslim friends I have, told me that Babangida isn't even a Nigerian! Hahaha.

#anyThingIsPossibleInNigeria. But back to Babangida's matter, it is known in Nigeria today, that Babangida sent a letter bomb to my hero Mr. Dele Giwa, just because Mr Giwa was investigating a drug deal, which Babangida's dearest wife was part of. Until today, the stolen $12.4billion oil windfall from the 1991 Gulf War has STILL NOT been accounted for.

Then we had the most foolish and idiotic Sani Abacha. He took power through a coup. Systematic violations of human rights, complacency towards drug trafficking and systemic corruption at all levels. Thanks to him Nigeria was EXCLUDED from the Commonwealth sometime in 1995, the same year I left Nigeria.

Why did the Commonwealth do this? The idiot hanged eight opposition leaders, which included Ken Saro-Wiva.

I personally feel that Abacha killed Nigeria because his corrupt practices became blatant and systematic. I can recall seeing pictures in the local newspapers of truckloads of cash. I wonder how the Abacha family can still live in honour. They should be ashamed to rant when their father's woes are remembered. They should even be apologizing and begging Nigerians to find a place in their hearts to forgive their stupid father. Sometimes it bothers me how this president Jonathan reasons, honouring a man like Abacha in a Nigeria where people that witnessed the Abacha oppression are still alive.

1993 was the year I passed my JAMB exams and had intentions on registering for my first year at the University of Benin. University enrolment back then was fucked up and the various teachers' unions were also constantly on strike. There were problems between old and new confraternities. Most of the confraternities reigned through oppression and fear. Some confraternities killed and raped fellow students in broad daylight. My brother's roommate was axed one evening whilst my brother was sleeping right next to his corner. Can you imagine this! In a university!

Universities and secondary schools were during Abacha's reign, just too unsafe. As an adolescent with a handful of "caught in-betweens" I opted for leaving the country instead of staying back and enrolling in the university and maybe getting myself killed. But there again, I had a handful of friends that enrolled back then and they were among the saviours.

Today Babangida, Obasanjo and Buhari are very alive, well and kicking. I call them the untouchables. Free as birds despite all the money they stole. No one can bring them to justice. This is the reality of life my fellow Nigerians and I have to live with. Nigeria in these past few weeks finds itself in the middle of the state and presidential elections that have just been postponed for six weeks. From past history, such periods have usually been tense and unpredictable. I hope and pray that things will be calm this time around. From the various discussions I have had with taxi drivers and people from various walks of life, I have come to understand that a number of Nigerians I've come across seem to be voting automatically for General Buhari and not the incumbent president, Jonathan, mainly because there is NO other better candidate. I find this sad!

I shall not vote because I feel Buhari and Goodluck are totally incapable of leading Nigeria. Goodluck for one is a very strange fellow. He was just credited a statement saying, "corruption is not stealing". Goodluck's term in office is just like a schoolboy who never passed primary one. Constantly failing. If Fashola were a presidential candidate, I would definitely vote for him. Why? Lagos reflects his credibility to rule.
In fact, to be candid, my Swiss side tells me to lead and deploy guerrilla warfare, a sort of coup d'état, which overthrows the current president. Yes, Nigeria needs a revolution!

60% of the poor population could constitute a tremendously potent revolutionary force. I can identify and map myself with most of the socialist ideas Che Guevara expounded. One of the beliefs he fought for was based on common ownership and collaborative decision-making. I respect Che Guevara for the fact that he believed in something and at the same time he was willing to fight and die for it.

Injecting such a revolution in Nigeria's population is possible through propaganda. But this will not be enough. We will also need citizens with a similar mind-set like me. The kind of mind-set, which makes people believe in something and are willing to die for it. But that is quite IMPOSSIBLE to find in Nigeria today. The current Nigerian mind-set I see today is more about: Every man for himself, God for us all. The Nigerian people have lost their beliefs and hope in their governments and rulers. Their wishes of the masses have been ignored and political promises recklessly abandoned. The Nigerian people feel abandoned and left alone. It is almost IMPOSSIBLE to regain their trust.

I believe Nigeria needs more than "one free meal a day in public schools". I believe Nigeria should create a place, for fellow Nigerians to be able to dream and plan their life. I believe Nigerians have a right to basic amenities such as running water and stable electricity. Starting with these basic amenities will lead to a domino effect of other relevant projects.

Las Gidi

As the most populous city in Nigeria, Lagos is one of Africa's most eclectic, chaotic mega-cities. It was named after the Portuguese word for 'lagoon' due to its geographical composition of islands and sand spits. It also has a turbulent political history and was stripped of its capital city status in 1991. However, Lagos still remains Nigeria's definitive city of culture. Lagos is also the home of my personal hero Fela Anikulapo Kuti, father of the Afrobeat movement.

It is exceedingly difficult to come up from nothing in this teeming city on the Atlantic. Still, every person who makes the decision to pack up their lives and maybe start anew in Lagos must believe they have the capacity to do just that. I for one had this in mind twelve years ago.

My night was quite HOT (25-30C plus humidity). I had a typical Nigerian NEPA deprivation. Due to the absence of electricity, I generate tonnes of heat, which keeps me awake at intervals.

Soon came Sunday morning and my sleep was rudely cut short (again) by the chanting pastor.

My week started out quite festive. I was invited to the marriage presentation of Chinedu's cousin in Ipaja, a densely populated area, to the west of Lagos.

There are a number of phases in a typical Nigerian traditional wedding. Every ethnic group defines exactly what they want in the various phases. But generally one shall always find these three phases: "knocking on the door", "asking" and the "traditional wedding".

I was invited to the "asking". We arrived the bride's home at noon. The bride's parents live in a brown bungalow situated on the outskirts of Ipaja. In front of their home were two canopy tents positioned opposite each other. The bride's family were already seated under the canopy erected beside a large mango tree. It was quite obvious to us that the other canopy was for the groom's family. Separating these two canopies was space and a large wooden table. Chinedu and his cousin stood up immediately to place their gifts, offerings and some bottles of liquor on the table. At exactly 12:30 the ceremony started.

A female MC in her late fifties led the ceremony. Chinedu's cousin's parents were invited to the space. They where asked to present their reasons for coming. After this was done, the MC led a series of prayer songs and chants. During this chanting we were all invited to make monetary donations three times in a role. Personally I was not a fan of the MC. She married words of money, God and prosperity a lot in her chants and sayings.

At the end of this ceremony, Chinedu's cousin's parents left with a wedding list and a wedding date. Whilst at the ceremony, thoughts came to my mind - images from back in the day when Chinedu and I were kids. We used to invite ourselves to all the wedding ceremonies in our neighbourhood. We had basically no idea what was going on, we were simply on site to eat rice and drink cold bottles of Fanta. Those were good times.

On our way to Victoria Island we were stuck in another long traffic jam. This time the cars were NOT moving. I think we sat in the car for like one hour before things started getting better. As we gained velocity, I coincidentally looked to my right. My eyes caught a female hawker falling backwards to the ground. As she dropped to the ground, I suddenly could tell she was actually having an epileptic seizure. I found myself caught in-between our moving car and a desire to help the hawker. I was totally unable to react. As we drove away I saw the lady vanish among the chaos. It's a pretty tricky dilemma - trying to help and get in trouble. Don't help and leave others in worse situations.

We opted for the Third Mainland Bridge, which led us directly to this posh side of Lagos. Victoria Island was once an Island before the water around it was covered with sand and eventually connected with a bridge. Here you get to meet the "other" Nigerians who spend 25$ dollars for a bowl of pasta with pesto. It has a contrast so stark that you could believe for one second that you're not in Nigeria. It mirrors the troublesome wealth divide between much of Africa and the West.

Ordinarily, residing in Victoria Island is a privilege. It should be, considering the fact that all along, only those belonging to the aristocratic class of the Nigerian society could afford to reside on this island. Despite the yawning prospects of a Tsunami by the nearby, Atlantic, the rich would prefer dying hard - breathing the fresh air that the ocean presents before passing it on to fellow citizens of Ajegungle, Mushin…oops, sorry, I almost forgot.
We were headed to the spiralling and now modernized Federal Palace Hotel. Located on the shores of the interface between the Atlantic and the Lagos lagoon, the historic hotel dominated the Lagos hospitality industry for a long time until it was forced into hiatus.

This hotel was initially called Victoria Beach Hotel in the 1950s, and was famously the setting for the signing of Nigeria's Declaration of Independence. This is another place I visit every time I come to Nigeria. I come here to see several elements of the original décor from the 70s, not least the historic boardroom that hosted the birth of an independent Nigeria.

Lagos to me symbolizes being at home in an irony of tranquillity amidst organized chaos. I have only been here for about two weeks and I must say that most of the warnings and cautionary tales about Lagos as a whole (both local and international) are nothing but an old wife's tales.

Lagos is large; Lagos survived the Portuguese in 1472, the British in 1861 and the Biafran War in 1967. Ebola has NO ROOTS in Nigeria. Patrick Sawyer, a Liberian-American who brought Ebola into Nigeria on July 20th 2014 later died in Lagos. I am proud to experience that Nigeria succeeded in containing Ebola very well. It is important to know that if Lagos is down, Nigeria as a whole is down. The containment of Ebola shows that Nigerians can get things done but ONLY, if they have NO choice!

Break or bake a cookie

Hmmm, where shall I begin? Thirty-eight years cannot be adequately captured in this book. Why do I say this? It is 38 years since my eyes first viewed this world. My mum's womb was too bumpy and I felt I lacked space so I started pulling on my mother's cervix. Before we knew it, it dilated at 11:30 am on a Wednesday morning in May! My Swiss mother was rushed to the hospital only to find out that the doctors and nurses were on strike! My mum stood in front of the closed UBTH gate holding her football-like tummy whilst shouting for help. There I was, already presented with my first ever "caught in-between"; would I die or would I be delivered?

A young Nigerian doctor walked towards my mum, grabbed my mum by her hand and told her: "Come with me, we are on strike but I shall put you through your active Labour." That's how with the help of 'Doctor Make Possible' I was born!

Since then, many a time I have cussed during my life journeys! I cussed about how little I really knew about practicality, and the lack of guidance in my life. Although I have no blame or resentment I must conclude that I received poor guidance while growing up.

It requires a good amount of humility, sobriety, and courage to live in a cultural confluence - of confusion - and of identity crises.

I have often pondered this confusion and each time I come to a conclusion. Life would be boring = Life becomes nothing. I was able to sport both the frown and the laugher lines with the help of expressional humour. The Nigerian broken English or the so-called Pidgin English gave me a medium where I could unleash and expresses my frustrations.

Thank you Great Britain (+ Portugal) "Broken" is a good way to describe a language born from the improper/innovative use of another.

Pidgin, or broken English, is the popular lingua spoken in parts of West Africa. The patois cuts across Nigeria, which is home to hundreds of languages, making it easier for millions of "we" Nigerians from different parts of the country to communicate. It is a phonological system on its own.

I love the Nigerian Pidgin English. It was erected from contingency; it sounds pretty cool, rhythmic and very light. It is a language, which initially existed between a few British and (or Portuguese) merchants and Nigerian traders as early as the 15th century. From my understanding, each variant of the Pidgin English is of course specially constructed to suit the need of the person using it.

I mean lets be frank! If someone greets you after a long and terrible day at work with "I welcome you" you might just frown. But if someone greets you with: "I *throway* salute" you might just end up smiling or burst into laughter.

I grew up with the Bendel variant of the Pidgin English, which on its own could be divided into eleven sub variants. I always loved Pidgin right from childhood. I constantly challenged by my father not to speak it but I always ignored his instructions. The fact that I was not thought the Edo language made me more eager at grasping the Pidgin language. The strangest and saddest moments during childhood were transformed to happy moments with the help of Pidgin English.

I can recall informing Chinedu about how I panicked the day I lost my chastity. I was basically shocked and almost traumatised. But Chinedu stood there and sensitized me with some very local anecdotes delivered in flawlessly comical Pidgin English. My awkwardness was turned into laughter. Pidgin helped me see the "funny or comical side" of things or situations. I started reflecting about what it meant to have a humorous perspective on life from the age of seven. I have been able to develop and evolve over the years. I even managed to inject this humour into the other languages I speak.

It is fun speaking Pidgin when you are angry, happy, fighting, flirting, in love or trying to impress a girl. To me, Pidgin converts any Nigerian communication barrier to a "neutral" platform, a social hub or a language factory. It helps me free myself from the hurdles of caught in-betweens I experience on a daily basis.

I would like to share just a few barrels of first-hand segregation, which I experienced both in Nigeria and overseas. Some of these situations were to my advantage, while I transformed the unpleasant ones into a comical moment for myself with me in the starring role.

- Growing up as child in Benin, I had a meat addiction, not just any kind of meat but Asolo meat, which was sold by a man riding a bicycle. The fact I was "white" made him sell me Asolo meat on credit. My debt spanned months if not years. In fact I can't even remember if I paid off all my debt. Nigerians who have eaten Asolo meat know how hard it is to get served meat on credit.
   [I BAKED A COOKIE]
- My seniors in secondary school always oppressed me because of my natural "looks". Apparently some of their girlfriends found me quite sweet and *boyfriend-able* or rather *fuckable* to be honest. It came a day when three guys with

whom I have had affairs with each of their own girlfriends seriously beat me up. I went home contemplating revenge. Came back the next morning with my area guy. The guy took concealed a handgun under his shirt, and accompanied me. Once I passed the gate entrance, I made my way to the boys' classroom. Told them they should please step outside the school compound, which they dumbly did. I stood beside my area guy with them standing opposite us. My area guy just raised his t-shirt. They understood the message.
[I BAKED 3 COOKIES]
- Holiday time. Destination: Switzerland. Arrived in front of the Swiss immigrations officer. I presented him my Nigerian passport. He looked at me and said, please step aside. I think I waited for about 7-10 minutes. During this time, other people passed me. When I felt I've had enough, I stood in front of him again, and as he frowned I quickly showed him my Swiss passport. He turned pale and was at loss for words, that he just made a hand gesture indicating that I was free to pass.
[I BAKED A COOKIE]
- I had just turned twenty. Received my invitation to join a compulsory three months *Rekrutenschule* (RS) which was planned for the mid winter season. Three weeks into our training, a bunch of us noticed that our squadron leader was a racist. Over the next few months, we (a

bunch of mixed Swiss) were constantly abated and scrutinized by him. We managed to maintain our hurt and frustration until the end of our camp. The night before we were despatched, we devised a plot to get even; we planned on pouring five cold buckets of water on our squadron leader while he was asleep. When the clock turned midnight. We left our rooms, headed straight to the kitchen to fetch water with some buckets. We ended up with seven buckets filled with COLD WATER. Ten of us departed for his room. Opened his door, five soldiers stood on the left side of his bed and the other five on the right side. Five more were standing at entrance to his room while five others guarded the main entrance. We were all set to pour water on him. The first two soldiers on the left and one on the right were responsible for holding him down after the first current of cold water was poured. My friend Jacques gave the command "Wasser links"; left side poured their buckets. Squadron leader shouted and tried resurrecting like Jesus but Soldier Mosses, Hans and Ruedi held him down. The second command was issued; "Wasser Rechts" We poured ours then dropped the buckets immediately and ran off.

[I BAKED 1 COOKIE BUT ALSO BROKE 50]
- It's Friday night in Bern, Switzerland. I was 21 years old, looking sweet and all dressed up. Standing at the bus stop in Bümpliz waiting for the next bus into

town. Suddenly a police car stops in front of me with blue lights. Two huge guys stepped out and walked towards me. They demanded to see my ID in their Bernese German language. I started faking it, acting as if I didn't understand a word they were saying. I even pretended as if I could not speak Swiss German. They insisted I come with them. When I felt I had enough, immediately after he asked a question, I replied in the Swiss German accent. They turned pale, presented their excuses to me, jumped into their car and drove off.

[I BAKED 2 COOKIES]

- My son's mother flew to Japan on a business trip. And Daddy was home alone with son enjoying the weekend. We decided to go to a nearby park. Barely left my *casa* twenty minutes, I was engaged into a discussion with a middle-aged woman. I attract attention when I am alone but I attract double the attention when I'm with my son. "Wow, your son is handsome, his eyes are GREEN!" I replied: "thanks". She continued conversing with me. She mentioned she had kids but they are probably my age now. Some were at Midpoint she said, and asked: "is he your son? I mean are you his father". I replied, "Yes I certainly am" I then went on, "Your daughter works in the restaurant round the corner." She replied, "Yes she does". I continued: "she is my son's

mother! She never told you! Wow how sad." I left her standing there.
[I BAKED A COOKIE]

- On business in Los Angeles. Presented my Swiss passport to the US immigration officer. He stared at me and said, "You don't look Swiss." I replied "really! I am a particular Swiss…" The officer replied "particular?" I said, "yes I am also a communist my mum is ½ Russian-Swiss!" I spent hours before I was released. Lucky for me, I was not SHOT!
[I BAKED A COOKIE BUT ALSO BROKE ONE]
- In the second-class compartment in the train, which departed Bern for Zurich. I was on a business mission to meet a Product manager of a company X. Thirty minutes into the trip; Swiss Immigrations officers walked through the wagon and randomly inspected identity cards. I watched them coming. As expected the stopped in front of me, presented their greetings and asked for mine. I greeted them and replied, "the white lady before me was not asked to show her identification! Why?" Officer replied, "I chose randomly." I retorted, "I shall only present mine if the lady presents hers." Officer stared at me, took a step back and invited the lady to present her identification, which she did. There after he came back to me. I then presented mine to the officer. As if that was not enough, Officer asked where I was headed; I replied: "the final destination of this

train." Officer then asked what was in my rucksack, I told him that's personal. Officer said he would just have to check it out. I replied, "Certainly not, you will need a warrant first." Officer was like, "are you joking Sir?" I said no, I handed him out my second identity card, which was my company's card from the Swiss Justice department. He collected it, looked at it and handed it back to me and left.
[I BAKED A COOKIE]

- On holiday in Nigeria. Presented my Nigerian passport to the Nigerian immigration officer. He stared at me and said, "You don't look Nigerian." I replied "really! Na true you talk, I even forge my pali (passport) for Obalende self" The officer replied "abeg, carry your wahala dey go…" We both laughed.
[I BAKED A COOKIE]

I can't help it. When I smell negative or positive segregation, I just have to react. Anyone who places me in my in-betweens ends up being offended, irritated, confused, frustrated, angry or whatever. I don't really care what happens even if it ends up being politically incorrect. I shall continue to bake cookies rather than breaking them no matter what the price is. For me, segregation is converted to a "live" comic strip with me as the main actor!

Come to think about it, this stubborn aspect of my personality reminds me of my astrological sign "Taurus". As a person born zodiac sign of Taurus, I can sometimes be unbelievably stubborn and inflexible in my personal approaches so much so that when the logical arguments do not suit me, I refuse to listen! I defend my stance by cracking a joke.

Here are a few of the funny Pidgin phrases I use and what they mean:
- You sweet, Omo (you are very beautiful)
- Come wack (come and eat)
- Alam don blow (the secret has been exposed)
- I beg maintain (please be calm)
- Make we yarn (lets talk)
- Katakata don burst (trouble has occurred)
- Wetin be your logo? (Identify yourself?)
- Shine your eye well well (be careful)
- Yawa don gaz (real trouble has ensued)
- Wetin dey sele? (What is happening?)
- You sabi? (Do you know?) Sabi is actually derived from the Portuguese word "saber", to know.
- She don vex (she is annoyed) Vex is derived from the latin word "vexare", annoy.

Middle Class

My every day sights of parts of Lagos comprise of images of the downtrodden citizens to the well to do, and obscenely rich citizens.

Lagos is a melting pot of these two categories and also anyone in-between them. On my way to one of the Shoprite flagship stores, I saw a child selling sachet water in a biodegradable plastic. The time was a few minutes shy of 10pm. I reckon he was not older than Femi, my son. He was striding the length of our car, shouting: "buy fresh cold water here". I ended up buying just a sachet of water so I could clear my conscience. Anytime I see child hawkers, I go nuts! My Swiss side wants to step out of the moving car, pick up the child and drop him at his parents'. While there, shout at his parents for letting their son stay so late outside. I mean the child never chose to be born! It was adults that made that decision. But at the end, my Nigerian side takes over the situation by remaining passive and accepting the fact that children hawking in traffic is something we've all grown accustomed to – a normal thing. Child hawkers seem to be an ever-increasing issue in Lagos, despite the government's measures and steps in curtailing this development.
The government planned on banning "Sachet

water" in 2013. I find this to be an unkind gesture to the very poor in Nigeria.
The three tiers of government manage the Nigerian water sector; this monopoly minus a culture of accountability produces a circumstance, which promotes the incompetence and bias so prevalent in the sub-sectors. I for one still believe, that water determines our daily health. As a child, my mum parboiled water overnight before filling it into bottles. These bottles where then placed in the fridge as drinking water. As of 2015, she still does this.

But back to my rumination on the Shoprite matter. Shoprite is a South African owned, fast growing and leading commercial retailer in Africa. It can be compared to the Parisian Lafayette or the Spanish El Corte Inglés. They have shops in most cities in Nigeria. Hearing about this place, made me think about Leventis PLC stores back in the 80's. As kids, sometimes we sought refuge from the burning Sun in the Leventis stores. We played with toys and read books. We never managed to actually finish any of the children books we started reading since we were always chased away by store security. So in a way, Shoprite was "Lenventis" reborn to me. Shoprite combines shopping, meeting point, bars, restaurants, clubs and singles meeting point. I personally find it quite an artificial place. Being there, walking around, doing window-shopping feels strange to me. Don't get me wrong but I would rather do my shopping in a more authentic environment like CMS or Balogun

Market.

All your commercial needs can be satisfied here if you accept their exorbitant prices. For example a Samsung LCD LED 43 inch TV is between 65'000 and 160'000 Naira that is within the 350 US Dollars to 900 US Dollars range. Most upper middle class Nigerians can buy their electronic appliances here but it is important to dissect the term "middle class" in Nigeria.

It is very difficult now to assert that Nigeria sits on poverty, or that Nigeria has no middle class. In fact, the term "working class" is seldom used. I actually hate using the word "class". It can be sometimes derogatory and classist. To me "classism" is the younger brother of "racism". I for one, am definitely not racist, I just want to throw some light on a country's 170 million population – a country whose principal export product is crude oil. A country blessed with ethnicity, beauty but plagued by corruption.

In the words of the young musician, Wiz Kid, back to the matter. Take for example the Empire State building in New York. Let us say, that the Nigerian middle class is the size of it.

Characterizing a "middle class Nigerian" as someone who consumes at least 400'000N (about 2,000 US Dollars) a month is somewhat false since this particular category might only make up 3-4% of the Empire State building. I am more interested in the "lower middle class" which makes-up 6-7% of the Empire State building.

This means we are definitely looking at a monthly consumption of less than 100'000N (which is about 500$). Everyone from this " lower middle class" and below are actually the real backbone of the Nigerian Economy.

It is important to note that a great majority of Nigerian elites in this middle class category also have a technical education, university degree, Master's or PhD background. 50% of people in this "lower middle class" category could buy a Samsung LCD LED 43 inch TV in Shoprite BUT they might end up buying it somewhere else where it will be cheaper.
After finishing our window-shopping, Chinedu and I decided on going to the cinema. I have never been to a cinema in Nigeria, so this was a great opportunity. Tickets went for slightly over a 1000N (which is about 6 US Dollars). The theatre was packed with the young and old. The Hollywood film we watched was not that interesting but I enjoyed the atmosphere and excitement of people in the theatre. I shall definitely come back.

Food

Ok I have had enough! I must write about Nigerian food! Damn, I love it. Just had something sweet, crispy, spicy and crunchy for lunch. What can this be? Plantains! Plantains can be served either as a snack, as part of a meal or as a meal. When you need something just to nibble, then have it as snack. When you need something to tuck-in your stash, have it as a meal.

Since I arrived, I have been having it mainly as part of a meal. I had it served with fried rice, plain Jollof rice or just simple white rice. Jollof rice is another dish that has an attractive and sumptuous taste. It is basically your regular rice cooked in a delicious tangy tomato sauce. Anytime I eat Jollof rice I reconnect with my childhood birthday parties moments.

There is also Party Jollof rice, which is quite different from plain Jollof rice, as it tends to be more delicious with the added smoky burnt flavour. Back then, anytime I was invited to a friend's party I always asked what was served! I only went if Jollof rice was served (Its out, now I have admitted it!).

In Lagos, I discovered quite a number of restaurants, where they serve very good food.

Restaurants such as Sweet Sensation and The Place serve various Nigerian delicacies. Sweet Sensations' fried rice accompanied with plantain and beef is my favourite.

Based on reasons bordering on personal hygiene, I never eat "swallows" in restaurants. Swallow is a word, which categorises the various Nigerian dishes like Pounded Yam, Eba, Semovita or Amala. These meals are usually served with their corresponding traditional soup.

The other day I was visiting Chinedu's friend in FESTAC town. We strategically arrived at Afam's home around noon. Chinedu told me that Afam's wife was a very good cook. Afam and his wife, Adamma, welcomed us into their humble home. We were not even seated when Adamma informed us that, they were about to eat. She asked if we would care to join them. I jumped up and said yes with pleasure. I had no idea what exotic delicacy was about to befall my sight. My eyes were greeted with an Eastern Nigerian dish called Abacha! The dish had the same name, as a former hated Nigerian president. To be candid, I am not a big fan of this particular former president, but this dish killed it! It was prepared with shredded cassava and stockfish. The dish was mouth watering.

Enjoying Nigeria's local cuisine is a must-do for any person visiting this fabulous country. Every tribe in Nigeria is well known for its particular traditional foods, which I for one, haven't fallen short of sampling, since I arrived.

Away from the hustle and bustle of Lagos is an oasis of calm and solitude called The Jazzhole. This spot x-rays a trinity of culture. Chinedu told me that, the Jazzhole was once an iconic record shop, a renowned bookstore and a cutting edge café, which started initially with the selling of vinyl's back in the 1980s.

I noticed, when it comes to personal eating habits, some of us have a magnetic attraction to rice, a staple food. It is easy and fast to prepare, doesn't cost much and keeps one full. However, it doesn't have all the necessary vitamins and nutrients needed for a healthy diet.

Trying to achieve and maintain a healthy lifestyle whilst in Nigeria was a priority for me. Most of the Nigerian delicacies could be quite fatty if not prepared with care.

Nevertheless, I must share my last Nigerian dream meal from the North. This dish is some sort of pudding made with rice and can be eaten with any soup. This same dish has antioxidant properties and is very rich in calcium and protein! Do you know the name?

If yes, reply to me via my tweeter handle @aostefan.

Driver's Licence

I revised my decision to renew my driver's licence in Lagos since I found out that there was a second and less cumbersome option for officially renewing ones driver's licence.

The prodigious task of going through the FRSC, takes at least a week if not more. The laws relating to the licencing of drivers vary from Switzerland to Nigeria. In Switzerland a driver will only be issued a valid licence, only after he has passed a driving test. I have been in possession of a Swiss driver's licence for twenty years now but I am not allowed to use it in Nigeria. How silly can this be?

Since I could not find my Nigerian drivers licence and I wanted to be able to drive once I reached Benin City, I opted for the less cumbersome renewal option. I contacted a VIO (Vehicle inspection officer), handed him the necessary documents (passport, passport photos) and 15'000 Naira cash. I got my renewed licence after 3 working days! Is this not crazy!

Am I proud of what I just did? Well yes and no. Yes as in: I can certify that I once had a valid driver's licence but just couldn't find it. Since the "Nigerian system" offers this option via a VIO.

No because, I am caught in-between the category of Nigerians that have connections and could afford most of the things they want just by paying for it. Not every Nigerian could pay the outrageous amount of money required to renew their licence. Well, I did this, and you may as well say I definitely took advantage of my position.

A week later, the VIO officer called me up and told me that my licence was ready.

Trying to dissect the term position without being a victim. A position is a random order enforced by either one's self or an external attribution. As a teen I typically placed myself in situations where I sometimes wished I hadn't. I started driving at the age of 16, without a licence. This was certainly done without the consent of my father, as he never understood the reason why I should be driving at an early age. The reasons why I started learning were simple. Understanding practicality, summer house and birthday parties. With support of a handful of driving friends I was able (with time) to command one of my father's white Volkswagen T3 manually. My undercover driving class slots were somewhat out of the ordinary. I drove while returning from school, the market, the car mechanic, tennis classes, karate classes and so on. In fact any opportunity was turned into a driving collaboration.

On one *Naijatic* evening, I was seated in our blue Golf on my way to a friend's birthday party. My elder brother was on the steering wheel. I told him I would like to drive, since I'd been learning how to drive for a while now. Without talking too much, my brother parked beside the road and handed me the car keys. I took command of the Golf and drove off manoeuvring through the streets of the GRA area. We headed straight to my friend's house where the party was. As I made a left turn off the airport road, we were halted by one of the most notorious and recognised symbols of the Nigerian every day corruption: random police checkpoints.

Standing in front of our broken golf bumper were two rugged looking police officers. The officer on the left ordered us to "...comot for moto" which we did. The interactions with these dubious men were about to unfold to a basic common spirit. The officer on the right said, "oyibos na una get naija but una go do weekend for us today." As he ordered me to get the documents of the car, he was busy searching the Golf. I handed over the particulars to the officer who was struggling with gravity.

He was drunk and could barely stand still. He immediately asserted to his colleague that the Golf was stolen without even having a look at the particulars I handed to him. My brother and I were totally angry by now, but we had no choice but to verbally challenge their assertions. This ended up in all of us steeping into the Golf and driving to the next police station. On arrival, the DPO interrogated us. Half an hour later my brother was handed out a written statement, which narrated our involvement in a car chase. The DPO concluded that since I was 17 my brother was the only one to be apprehended and released on bail. We stood there with nothing but frantic expressions. Before we could react to this elaborate scheme, my brother was taken to a one-man cell. I panicked and ran out of the police station shouting for help.

ATM's and Network issues

I am in the middle of my second week in Lagos, and I must say that I am not too happy with bankcards, ATM's and email notifications. It's over eight years now since ATM's were introduced in Nigeria. 40% of the time I can't withdraw cash from an ATM or use my Bank X Verve card to pay via a POS (Point of Sale) facility mainly because of network issues/software issues.

I recently went to a Bank X ATM on Allen Avenue Ikeja, to withdraw 5000N. Halfway through the transaction; I was greeted with the message "transaction can't be processed at the moment". I had to abort the process and my card was ejected from the ATM machine. Later that afternoon, I received an email notification, which stated 5'000N was debited from my account. I was angry! I said to myself, what is happening here? Chinedu stared at me and laughed. He told me to calm down. Chinedu told me that the transaction would be reversed, and my account should be credited with the debited sum of money within twenty-four hours. I had difficulties in believing this. From a professional point of view, there is a problem with the realization of the whole ATM software approach. A client should ONLY get an email notification if his account was actually debited. The client is NOT interested in

wrongful/aborted transactions. A client should be able to retrieve cash from an ATM, and the client should also be able to print out a valid receipt of his transaction.
To cut the long story short, 24 hours later, I got another email notification, stating that; my account was credited with 5000N. Bad start but I'm glad it ended well. Many customers are usually not as fortunate.

What I like about Nigerians is their ability to convert any situation into an opportunity. The waiting lines in front of ATM's could be sometimes quite long. I always wondered why people took so much time to withdraw cash. I eventually found out that the cardholder usually had three to four other bankcards from either friends or relatives. Interesting how trust goes a long way. Nigerians are very sociable people; they have the ability of turning any situation into a social gathering.

The weeks that followed only added more frustrations to my Naija banking experience. This led me to create another account with a different bank. This did not solve any of my banking problems. Hence the symptom is different from the problem.

CMS

It was a Tuesday morning I was sitting beside the window in Chinedu's office browsing the Internet. Through the window, I could see a primary school. Parked in front of it was an old yellow Americana school bus. The exact type you see in the movie Nightmare on Elm Street. I also saw a large group of children playing; covered with red sand. Intriguing, isn't it?

I loved growing up in Nigeria. I had a lovely experience and as a parent, I would so love my children to experience the pleasures of growing up in Naija (broken English expression for Nigeria). Growing up was RAW (just the way I like it!). It was about dancing in the tropical rain, unity and friendship, building your toys out of cans and plastic, rolling truck tires down hill. My mother hardly understood why I hardly played with LEGO toys. I preferred building toys with Chinedu. I always enjoyed the togetherness, the cultural exchange.

Childhood Sunday mornings were all about going to Chinedu's home to "taste" the lunch that was already prepared by his mother, in her absence! I can still remember the delicious taste of the sauce with the beef swimming in it! Good times. Our parents did a fabulous job in bringing us up. Thank you mother and father.

Chinedu proposed we took the afternoon off and do some shopping. I said "hell yeah!" En route to CMS (Church Missionary Society), we listened to Usher's 'Good Kisser', with heads bumping to the music, only to be greeted with a one-hour traffic. Real traffic in Lagos is not slow moving cars but rather rooted cars, stuck for hours. There is a saying in Lagos that goes: "Maturity only comes through traffic jams!"

CMS is situated in the Bariga district of Lagos, the same district that has produced top African clergymen for decades. Driving down the bridge to my right I saw a semi submersible Oil Rig! I was surprised. WTF is this doing here? I WhatsApped my friend Zvezdin in Lausanne, told him about what I saw. Zvezdin replied "tell them to wait for me, I'll be there! Lol". I actually thought the militants were at work.

CMS is home to the oldest printing and publishing press in Nigeria (founded in 1913, I think). It was 2pm and we were walking past a Mallam's kiosk. At the same time I was observing the horde of people walking in a clustered form. The atmosphere was hot, humid and frantic. It was like a ritual. Left, Right, Forward, Backward. Reminding me of a Fela Kuti song. Suffering and Smiling. From bus conductors yelling out their destinations to a small party of 15 singing praises of God without restraint. Everyone was efficient.
As we continued our "waka" (or walking, as you would say in the West), I heard someone shout,

"Chairman, how far?" Chinedu looked ahead and smiled. As Chinedu replied "na package ohh", he whispered to me: "that's Peter", the trader we came to meet. Peter stood at the corner of his shop, he had well-polished shoes, with laces smartly tied into the shape of the number, 8. Peter invited us in. Peter's shop is situated in one of these old colonial buildings. It measures about three-meters by two square foot. There was no air-conditioning, only a ceiling fan. His shop was packed with cloths everywhere; up down, left, right and under.

Chinedu sat on a stool and I on solid pile of folded jeans. Most of Peter's cloths are directly imported from Mainland China. I tried out a couple of jeans, t-shirt and actually found three pieces I liked. I whispered to Chinedu, asking how much it was. He responded, "I don't know but I will give him 5,000 naira".

I was dumbfounded. Chinedu handed out the money to Peter. Peter took the money and counted it. Not to my surprise, Peter shouted "Oga mi, no be so". Peter wanted 4000 Naira additional.

Meanwhile, as the price battle was going on, I was busy trying out other things. It took us 30 minutes before we all came to an agreement. We concluded and I paid and as I was just about to leave, Chinedu told me, he would have paid 2000 Naira less, if I were not around. I exclaimed in anger. "What?"

I went back to Peter and rained fireworks of

curses at him. I was pissed again, the Taurus part of me took over again. I simply hate it when I have to pay more for stuff just because I am mixed or have a lighter skin. Peter stood there shocked. I ordered him to either give me all my money back or refund two thousand. Chinedu told me to calm down, but I refused. Chinedu insisted and advised again, I looked at Chinedu and said, "Ok."

On our way back to the car, Chinedu told me, "if you act this way every time I take you to buy stuff, I wouldn't have any seller ready to see me again." Just as my anger died down, I received a sudden phone call from London! It was Chidi the other childhood friend of mine calling. I've known him since the age of twelve. Since then we've shared a lot, rolled a lot and cried a lot too. Chidi told me that he should be in Lagos at 7pm tonight and asked if we fancied a meet up in Victoria Island. I said yes! We quickly made our way home to freshen-up.

Onikan

I visit the National Museum Onikan, Lagos every time I find myself in Nigeria. I was not surprised to discover that Nigeria was on total display. Being a lover of the arts, who has visited many museums in Paris, Rio, Hong Kong, London, South America and Asia, it was a trip that I had eagerly awaited. I mainly come back and hope for a better or rather differential experience.

My first observation was a differential gate fee category for foreigners. There were three categories of entry tickets for children, adults and foreigners. This is needless in a museum in a country like Nigeria that is trying to promote tourism. Categorising tickets for children and adults should suffice. More so, when citizens don't really have effective IDs, how could they be sure of one's nationality?

I could also observe that the environment was typically unkempt and the whole place appeared totally abandoned. The walls could certainly use a fresh coat of paint.

I usually walk straight to see the car in which Gen. Murtala Mohammed was in, when he was assassinated. Our lack of maintenance culture was boldly displayed. The car is still not maintained or cleaned. I am quite sure that

Gen. Murtala must have done a 360 flip in his grave.

If well managed, cultural tourism is a growing aspect of tourism, which attracts millions of people to throng into Nigeria, to observe our cultural facilities, which includes museums.

This is yet another example of how we, Nigerians, and as individuals, do not value or appreciate our own history and culture. People without value for their own history and culture are doomed for extinction, or at best, doomed for relegation to the dustbin of history.

Bank Y

After I continued having numerous issues with my bankcard, which was issued, by bank X, I eventually gathered enough courage to have a second attempt with another Nigerian bank, Y. I gathered the necessary documents and passport photos needed and made my way to Allen Avenue in Ikeja. There I stood by the roadside with my hands hanging out like a hiker. Since Bank Y was about a 20 minutes from Chinedu's office I decided to take either a bus or "keke", whichever one stops or comes first.

The Keke is a tricycle modified to carry passengers, usually 4 people. They look exactly like the ones we find in Thailand only less beautiful. Clearly, the keke is fast becoming the preferred means of public transportation in Lagos. Keke is like Okada, but goes a step further by providing shelter and balance.

To my surprise a keke stopped. Driving the keke was a grouchy guy who ordered me to jump in quickly. There was already another man in front beside the driver, a man and a woman seated behind. I had no other option than to squeeze myself into the 3rd position at the back. The lady seated behind had such a mighty Ikebe super that I barely had space to place my tiny butt on the seat.

I tend to notice that our Nigerian ladies have serious Ikebe super, something impossible to ignore! Ikebe is the Pidgin English word for "Buttocks". Unlike Kim Kardashian, Nigerian women don't have that need or craze for large buttocks. They need no silicon injection or any other form of butt lifting. They are naturally born with it. All they have to do is wear the suitable or rather inappropriate dress.

The Ikebe lady accompanied us for about ten minutes. The funny thing was when she stepped out of the keke. Everyone stared at her Ikebe. Watching her vanish into the crowd reminded me of the famous viral comic magazine back in the 80's that baffled the whole society. I remember buying weekly copies, just to read the adventures of its slapstick characters. The magazine wasn't political, neither was it religious; it was mainly humorous. It had a genuine way of making light of every situation, being trivial and yet non-offensive.

The keke driver drove off whistling and singing. I reckon Ikebe made him happy. Luckily for me the ride lasted only about 15 minutes.

Getting to the bank's main entrance, there was a queue. The bank's point of entry and exit was made of two walk-through tube-like cylinders with sliding doors integrated in them. Something similar to the ones you find in the United States at security control points. The only difference with these ones was that they have no particular scan function. A security guy standing in front of the tube with a body scanner does the scanning. Body scanners should provide an additional layer of security but it was used as the principal and only layer of security.

After I was scanned, the security guy asked me to walk through the tube. Once in the bank I made my way up to the first floor where I asked the security guard to point me to the next available bank clerk. He pointed me to a table. There I found a middle-aged man sitting on his desk. He was packaged in a pair of black shortened ankle pants with a red dress shirt, knotted with a long tie.

He greeted me with a smile and automatically handed out 2 forms to be dully filled. I took the forms, taxied myself into a waiting room, down the aisle.

The bureaucracy in the two banks I have visited was quite overwhelming. 70% of the work is still done by paper and hand. The whole process of opening an account is quite tedious. It took me 20-25 minutes to fill the forms.

Walking in the bank, I just couldn't stop noticing the hairstyles of Nigerian women. I know I am about to touch a very sensitive topic and I also know that fashion aficionados would brush me aside as a novice. But I find wigs, Cotonou hair, Ghanaian hair or even Brazilian hair on Nigerian women a total disaster!

History never told us that for a person to be certified "a woman", she must have long hair. How come most Nigerians and Africans believe that they should have long hair? A significant percentage of black women today have subscribed to ignorance and sometimes insensitivity about how they actually look in and outside the black community. I am a big fan of Afro textured hair. I also enjoyed seeing my grandmother with her natural short white hair. As far as I know, my grandmother never braided her hair. There are so many hairstyles that could be worn on such a hair texture. I don't seem to understand why Nigerian ladies want to look like other women instead of just being their selves. Putting on fake hair is not really being accepting oneself.

I don't seem to understand why most Nigerian women have this intense desire to be caught in-between Afro textured hair and European long hair. Be you, stay yourself. I am a big fan of the Benin female activist Mrs Jane Osagie! She is a lady with very strong personality packaged naturally in her Afro textured short hair.

After work

After work, I decided to stop by at a top bar in G.R.A. There I met up with some old friends Osama and Ire. They just flew in from Thailand. We ordered a couple of beers and chatted a bunch. One time during the course of the evening, Osama brought out some pills. He asked us if we wanted to leave for the next level and we all said yes. Each of us took a pill, placed it in our mouth and flushed it with a cold glass of Star beer. We continued chatting for a while, speaking about secondary school, our teachers, parenthood and life as an adult. Before, I knew what was happening, it was already close to midnight. Since I was not in Lagos, I decided it was high time I left.

I was alone, walking towards my car, which was not parked in the parking lot due to lack of parking space. My car was packed outside, just around the corner of the Benin Golf course. As I was about to open my car door, I heard footsteps behind me. As I turned to see, a cutlass was pressed against my throat. A man covered my mouth with his hand, and whispered not to shout. He then took me to a car parked nearby and shoved me into the floor of the backseat and waved the cutlass at me, reminding me not to shout or say anything. He was skinny, wearing a blue t-shirt, had a thick moustache and short hair; approximately 6 foot; mid-30s, and spoke with a noticeable Igbo accent.

At this moment, a second man appeared. He was also in his mid-30s. He was wearing a native striped shirt, had a crew cut, and spoke with a Benin accent. He grabbed the car keys from the Igbo guy and demanded for my wallet. I couldn't remember where it was. They pushed me deeper into the car with their feet, and the Igbo man got into the back seat with me. The Benin man got into the driver's seat and drove off.

I asked them what they wanted. But at that point they didn't even reply or ask for anything. Instead, the Igbo guy dialled up a number on his phone. He seemed to be speaking about some kind of meet up. Then it hit me. "Oh my God. Oh my God. This is really happening. I'm being kidnapped and I think I know what they want". My heart exploded in panic, I got totally confused for a couple of seconds, I had a feeling I was deaf. The Benin guy seemed to be asking me something, but I could only hear my heart beat.

I started quivering and shaking in fear. I was so afraid. I thought I was going to die. I was weak with fear and deathly afraid. For a moment, I thought, "This was it". Suddenly the thoughts of my sons and loved ones came to my mind. I told myself, if I don't do something now there would be a far worse fate in store for me. It was the third time in my life I actually felt not caught in-between something.

So I forced myself to look around and see if there was any way I could escape. The car made a sharp curve, which prompted me to place my hands on the seat. My right hand touched a sort of pen or something, which was situated on the edge of the seat.

And then I waited. I knew that the car would have to slow down at some point in time, as it exits to merge with the main Airport road. The moment it slowed down, I picked up the pen or what ever and stabbed it continuously into the jaw of the Igbo guy! He started screaming and shouting for help! The driver looked back shouting "Guy u don die oh". I removed the pen and stabbed it twice into the right lower part of the driver's neck. By this time there was blood gushing everywhere. Everyone got hysterical; the driver lost control of the car, which started swerving from left to right. The Igbo man was screaming for his life and I was busy punching him on the face. At this point, the car, which was about to enter the Ring Road roundabout, skidded straight and crashed into the Benin museum fence. I was still dazed from the crash, but I opened the car door and tried to make a run for it. I failed. I kicked my legs out of the car, but the Igbo man had managed to pull my body back in. From that moment on, everything was a blur. I remember the driver, leaning over the front screen unconscious. At that point I remember thinking, "Even if I don't get out now, I need to keep the door open and my legs out the door. At the very least, it should cause a scene, and someone would see me.

So I continued kicking. My right foot pushed against the wide-open car door to keep it open. I recall elbowing, struggling, kicking, and even biting fingers. I lost my cool, and was struggling blindly for my life. At some point due to weakness the Igbo man loosened his grip. I made a jump out of the car, and ran far and wide.

I was hysterical, I ran very quickly in panic back towards Airport road. At some point I made a left turn. I stopped for a while and looked at the building in front of me, it was the Golf course. I was surprised to have reached there already. I had the feeling I was not even running for so long. So I decided to make a tangential cross via the manicured grass of the Golf course. As I stepped foot on the grass, I felt a relief and liberation, running over the grass with only half a pair of my shoes on my right foot.

I did not stop until I got to my car. When I finally got there, I placed my hands in my right pocked only to find out it was empty. I was searching relentlessly for my car keys and wallet. Suddenly someone called me: "Oga!" I looked back. It was the bartender from the bar. He shouted "Oga you forget your keys and wallet for here".

I made my way back into the bar. When I entered, looked at the table where I was seated. I was surprised to find my wallet and my car keys. As I walked closer to pick them up, I stumbled on something with my left feet. The object was the other half of my pair of shoes lying under the chair.

Damn, I must have taken the red pill. Red pill awareness, like most radical changes in life, made me believe I was actually struggling for my life when it was just a dream!

Next time I take the blue pill instead.

God is Good

Today marks two weeks and two days since I arrived Nigeria. This morning I was thrown out of bed not by a fabulous singing priest but rather by my Nexus 5 alarm clock.

Today is the day I planned travelling to Benin by road. Benin city is my birthplace and is situated to the north of Lagos.

For two weeks I struggled within myself whether to hit Benin by road or go by air as I had already embarked on various journeys this far in Nigeria. I was filled with "Naija adventure syndrome" like my close friends would call it. Now the moment of decision had come I said to myself. I planned to travel by road mainly because I am not that confortable with planes in Nigeria despite the fact that, air travel is amongst the safest in the world. I for one believe that Nigeria is not part of the world.

I got up as early as 5am so as to arrive at the bus station of God is Good at Yaba in Mainland Lagos by 6am. Most national and private bus services are baptised with either names or quotes from the bible. Funny.

God is Good proposes various buses for trips to Benin. Among these, were buses that waited until all seats where filled up with passengers before they departed. I call this option Las Gidi style. Another option was taking the "early bird", which departs exactly at 6:30am.

On arrival at 6.45, I was so lucky to meet the last seat available. And so we took off for the unending journey, from Yaba Park to Benin.

Moving from one village to the other was so much fun. I saw people of different shapes and sizes and heard people speaking different languages. As the hour went by, we crossed over a handful of communities and even by then we had barely gotten to half of the journey of estimated 400km. We were then still trapped along the lonely 200km Lagos - Ore 3 hours after. This segment of the highway could be the worse in the whole country, which has accounted for a lot of accidents. The segment is so bad that 70% of the cars coming from Lagos drive on the same lane as the oncoming traffic from Benin. Imagine this - cars, trucks and motorcycles driving at speeds of 120km/h on the same lane. The longer we travelled on this shared lane, the more I got nervous and stressed out.

Before I knew what was happening, I dozed off in the bus until I heard a loud noise from a little child hawker "Buy your cold water here" then I woke up, I looked around and discovered the bus driver stopped at a petrol station to buy some petrol. Surprised, I stayed close and glued to the window beside me to be double sure it was indeed a petrol station. I suddenly jumped out of the bus and went to the toilet.

The road segment from Ore to Benin was perfect. Cars drove on the correct side of the expressway. The rest of the journey went smooth and passengers discussed the on-going presidential elections and Bollywood movies.

Then finally we arrived at Ugobwo Gate, which is the junction linking to the University of Benin. 50 meters further down the road was the University of Benin Teaching Hospital, the place I was born. Only then I realized, I was now in O'vie Edo!

At the bus station in Iyaro, Benin, I jumped on a cab, which drove me to my family home. At the height of Ikbopa slope, I saw a crowd gathered round the lifeless body of a lady. I was flabbergasted. Mr Taxi driver told me, she has been lying there for 24 hours already. This is yet again the classic "Observation process" in which I find myself without the power of choice.

No one wants to be caught in the middle of another man's misfortune which is why you will see someone being beat up on the street, hear a voice calling for help in the bush, or see a dying man lying by the side of the road and ignore them because the last person who took a dead man he found dying on the road to the police station ended up being held as the prime suspect in his death.

A while later, I arrived at he junction of my street. As I walked towards the house, Mrs Bola, the caretaker who had been monitoring my movement via phone calls, was waiting at the gate to receive me. We exchanged pleasantries before I made my way upstairs to my room…

It's great to be home!

Benin, a decaying City

My first night in Benin was blessed with NEPA once again. I had no moments of electricity the whole night. The weather was very hot and the generator was defunct. Over 5 different churches laid siege on my sleep at 4 in the morning with loud speakers. The morning breeze swayed the various chants and recitals of the independent pastors past my room window. I encountered difficulties in continuing my sleep despite the fact that Morpheus touched my eyelids with his golden wand.

Back to my Benin things, I am a Benin boy; my Benin name is Osagibovo, which translates to "God is not jealous". My fabulous grandfather gave the name to me shortly before he passed away. Most of my uncles, aunties and other family members see me as a reincarnation of my grandfather. I am a very big fan of my grandfather! I sometimes wish I had spent some precious time with him. My grandfather served as the personal translator of Oba Akenzua II of Benin. Everything about Benin is woven around the Oba. The Oba is the pivot on which the activities in Benin rotate starting from the day-to-day salutations, even identifications of human beings and periods are linked to the Oba.

Stefan Asemota *Caught In-between*

Years back I visited the Oba's Palace during the Igue Festival. The Bini have a long lineage of Obas, and Igue is also an occasion to celebrate Ugie-Evhoba among other festivities. During this period, the Bini celebrate the anniversary of their deaths, and for seven days, propitiations are made to the spirits of the departed Obas. This is done to invoke their blessing on the reigning monarch and on their family and subjects. Lovely, isn't it?

I walked into the palace with other family friends and took our seat under a canopy. The canopy was placed to the right of the Oba of Benin. His royal highness, the Omo N' Oba N' Edo Uku Akpoloko Oba Erediauwa was sitting in his chair enjoying the festivities. His presence transmitted a strong aura of *Zenitude*. It was actually the first time I saw the Oba. I enjoyed stealing glances at him once in a while during the festival. It was a fantastic feeling being in the presence of the grandchild of the Omo N' Oba N' Edo Uku Akpolokpolo Oba Ovonramwen, the last independent Oba in the Benin Kingdom. He confronted the British, which led to the war of 1897 and was deported by the British, to Calabar where he lived in exile. Come to think of it, it was stupid! Imagine being exiled in your own country run by foreigners! It can be compared with having to banish the Queen of England to Tanzania for insubordination! Damn, I wish I could do this. A better analogy would be to colonize the United States of America, introduce African Religions, burn the White House and desecrate all the historical artefacts. Same as they did in Benin back in 1897!

Back to the matter, on one occasion, the Oba looked to his right and fixed his eyes on me while I was looking at him. I froze. His scrutiny was so intense; I felt my heart beat hard and fast.

The Oba called for one of his servants. Spoke to him a bit. The discussion with his servant resulted in the boy walking towards me. I became totally nervous. At one point I wanted to be the Wizard of Oz and disappear. But since that was not possible, I was rooted in my seat. The last time I could recall being so nervous was when I was waiting for my JAMB results.

The servant walked up to me and asked me: "what family are you from? Who is your father?" It was quite visible that I was the only light-skinned person around. So I answered: "my father is the son of Adu Asemota." He replied, "ok". The servant returned to the Oba and whispered in his ear. The Oba smiled and spoke with the servant, which, again, resulted in him coming back to me.

I was like "damn! What's up?" The servant walked up to me and said: "The Oba sends his greetings to your dad" and then went on to say that my dad has not been to the palace in ages. I was dumbfounded, speechless that the Oba knew my father's name. The servant told me to enjoy my time.

I love traditions and I love the history of Benin City until just before I was born. But there again I find myself stuck with the Edo language that I cannot speak.

Done reminiscing, it was time to go out and rediscover Benin! As I said earlier, I was born and bred in Benin. I know Benin as good as the back of my hands. I just could not wait to jump into the car to see my favourite places and spots. Among my top three places are the Oba's Palace, the Benin museum (there is only one, you cannot miss it) and the Ramparts/Moats (called Iya).

My grandmother once told me that the first European travellers to reach Benin were Portuguese explorers in about 1485. She also told me that some residents of Benin City spoke a pidgin Portuguese language in the late 19th century.

Back then our forefathers understood the essential nature of a planned city. They therefore planned streets with houses facing each other and footpaths leading to their farmlands and at strategic intervals, they created open spaces for meetings of the elders and playgrounds for the youths. In addition to planning, they engineered unique drainage systems that stood for centuries. The drainage system now known as the Benin Moat was a marvel to people from far and wide. The Benin Moat also served as initial buffer, and defence against the British invaders in the same war of 1897. Coincidentally, it is the most prominent landmark and perhaps the more noteworthy tourist attraction that Benin is known for besides the Bronze Artworks.

But the Benin I saw in the weeks to come had nothing to do with its history. It even had no comparison with the times I lived and schooled. If my grandfather could see Benin today, he would be turning in his grave.

The traffic is now MADNESS, the Binis are mostly very fast-talking, loud and somewhat aggressive at times. Manoeuvring a car through Edo newly congested roads is worse than the days I lived here.

The most worrisome part of this decay is that nearly every street has shops for traders and hawkers who are a nuisance to people who reside on these streets. Take my road for example; often there is loud music blaring from speakers strategically placed for maximum noise effect. No attention is being given to try to curb the environmental hazards that these activities pose to residents. Worse still, houses near my home are being turned into churches and one wonders whether permits are sought before these houses are converted either to religious or commercial buildings.

As if all this was not enough, for a couple of years, Benin City has been notorious for being the major source of victims of trafficking for purposes of sex work in Italy and other Western European countries. I saw Jane Osagie (the lady with real short Afro hair) of the International Reproductive Rights Research Group (IRRRAG) the other day at the post office. I almost ran to her for an autograph. Most of her NGO's anti-trafficking activities involve prevention and education. One of the results of her recent research stated that out of 32 victims of trafficking interviewed in Edo and Delta States, more were introduced to sponsors by parents or relatives than by agents or friends. Some parents, seeing another family's growing wealth after a daughter has been sent abroad, actually seek out sponsors for their daughters.

The Edos are lovable people but I can't stop noticing that they seem to have a tight relationship with their mobile phones; from working colleagues taking selfies and photos of each other in their offices to Okada riders texting while riding at the same time. Everyone seems to be totally connected to at least one or two phones at the same time. I personally find this sad. If the Edos continue at this pace, they will certainly become less lovable and socially detached.

There is a Benin proverb that goes: "Ore avbiere a mue no mwentin la" which loosely translates to: "you parade the strong through the neighbourhood of the weak and cowards."

I think the Edos are far from this.

Which is the way forward?

Wudu

My sweet grandmother was a Yoruba Muslim. The first of ten wives my grandfather married, spoke five different languages fluently. She practiced Islam for certain beliefs. When her expectations were not met, she switched to the Nigerian traditional religion thus hold to one and despise of the other (Order is reversible). I can still remember her singing chants in Islam and at the same time throwing two raw eggs to the street every evening at 6pm.

I have been exposed to Christianity and Islam right from birth and I can assert that there has always been harmony. Neither Christian nor Islamic teachings were flogged and drummed into my ears. I was never prompted by my father to choose either the Christian or Muslim faith.

I was first exposed to Islamic prayers when I visited one of my father's friends over the Ramadan period. The "call to prayer" just got into my spirit. It fascinated me and at the same time brought shivers down my spin. Years later, at the fine age of eighteen, I left for Lagos to learn German at the Goethe Institute in Victoria Island for a year. I stayed with my father's friend who was born in Kano. After his studies he later moved to Lagos to work for a then well-known bank. He practiced and followed the teachings of Islam.

I initially found the call to prayer five times a day a bit crazy and it almost drove me mad. But after a week, I basically fell in love with it. I was kind of spiritual and dedicated.

As the weeks rolled by, I developed an intense intellectual and mystical thirst, in trying to understand the various practices. So one Friday afternoon, I asked my dad's friend if I could come along with the family to the mosque for prayers. He looked at me stunned but replied, "certainly, if you wish".

Arriving at the mosque, a multitude of people of different age categories were squatted in front of the prayer hall doing the "Wudu" – the ablution. Ablution is the ceremonial washing of the body before an act of prayer. I was told that this was the primary key to prayer, the key to paradise. After I was apprenticed on how to execute an ablution, the Muezzin recited the "adhan". We made our way immediately towards the main entry of the mosque. Removed our shoes and walked in. The tiles inside the mosque were cool and fresh. Walking bare foot was just fantastic.

The position of the Muezzin in a mosque can be compared to that of a Christian verger except that during the call of prayer he faces the Kibla. His chanting was melodious; I believe anyone could hear his strong voice from miles away. The prayer sessions and recitals lasted about forty-five minutes.

During the next six months that followed, I developed a deep interest in understanding the teachings. I was adept in the art of recitals and chants. I actually got to the point where I wanted and even planned on converting to Islam. I found myself, yet again, caught in-between conversion to Islam and my dad. I was worried about what my dad would have said had I told him about my intentions. I eventually decided not to convert to Islam.

My one-year with this great family encompassed acts of worship, the doing of good deeds to all living things and the opposition to injustice. One of the teachings that I took home with me is a belief in a single, unitary God Who is all-powerful, all knowing, and without any children or family of any kind. My religious thoughts today depict this single belief.

How it all goes down

Home is an ambivalent word for me. I portray another "idea" of home. Due to this fact, I had no "emotional nest" to return to at night. With time I evolved into being a lonely soldier. I have felt like a misfit for most of my life mainly because of the fact that as of now, I still don't have definitive answers to the following questions:

1. **Who am I?**
   My chocolate soft toned, smooth skinned enhances my physical appearance a lot. This makes me, stand out from the crowd. I am basically "colour locale" anywhere I go, or anywhere I be.
2. **Whose side am I on?**
   Whilst growing up, parental conflicts created "sides" which sometimes related to racial issues.

"How to believe in one self?" has always been the question I asked myself ever since. This question is not quite trivial and God, Allah, or any other spiritual high can't even help me on this one. My separation/ divorce was the straw that broke the camel's back. I totally lost the notion of how to believe. I had a very LOW esteem of myself as a partner and father. With time, I learned how to "see through myself". Meeting "other persons" helped me in understanding my faults / weakness. Accepting these was sometimes very hard and painful. I still sometimes have "flashbacks" related to my faults.

My trip to Nigeria exploded some very crucial points, which were:
- "Standing up for what I want", which relates to the question: What does Stephan want to fulfil with regard to who am I and which side am I on.
- How can I resolve my hellish purgatory of in-betweens?

I am a person that functions better with "existential security". I am aware of my greatness and the positive effect/impact I have on people especially women. But this can never guarantee me existential security.

Today my fear and misunderstanding from my past relationships have become my wisdom; my greatest mistakes are no more permanent. Man, woman or we humans. We all live and grow everyday. In this one life, our humanity, a humanity we all share at the depth of our souls, deserves respect. As imperfect beings, we don't respect our own or anyone else's humanity absolutely. So when we fight, our partners are actually asking us to "update our software" (grow up/learn/evolve".

Perfection is nice BUT real is better. Why? Because perfect "does" not exist. Real is doable, anyone can "strive" towards anything. The trick in any partnership or relationship is discovering someone that has the same imperfections as you have. Hence deleting my "perfection" expectations allowed me to "meet" the other.

Self-belief is vital. Life is my best teacher. I was a young guy on the block at the Montreux Jazz festival totally disconnected and endowed when suddenly "that lady" walked in my "chant de vision" unexpectedly. I have experienced such moments only three times in my life. It was one of those moments where I had to get my mind on my side. I only had about 7 seconds of my life to decide weather I should create the moment or not. I believed she earned it. We live with no lies and her "imperfections" just turn me on! She teaches me how to believe **WITHOUT PROMISING.** I want this now! Me like it!

Rewind to existential insecurity. Nigeria. We can feel insecure in several practical dimensions: financial, physical, social, interpersonal, and emotional. But a much deeper level of insecurity, which is existential insecurity, cannot be solved by any of the security-operations that will resolve our ordinary worries about not being safe enough.

Not knowing how safe your child is in school or a country still trying to retrieve the missing Chibok girls after a year basically says it all.

Nigeria is like me, totally fragmented. It is totally showered in tribalism and cultural issues since the first day, that "stupid human being" stepped foot on our soil. Our idiotic past and present leaders are still not willing to "Do". Yoda's most memorable quote: "Do or do not, there is no try" is one of my favourite quotes. Nigerian has been trying since 1960 and we are still not "doing" it.

My experiences these past few months in Nigeria made me understand (again) that the majority of people couldn't see beyond my race, whether they had romantic, platonic or whatever interests. Despite my "skin" colour, I was able to integrate my identities linguistically, socially and cognitively without defragmenting myself.

But my last trip from Benin to Lagos really hit the nail on my fragmenting / defragmenting abilities. I was made to understand that existential insecurity was just a blanket that we humans can never control.

Barely a few minutes after jetting past Ore we suddenly noticed there was no incoming traffic coming from Lagos. Our swift driver noticed this verbally and started slowing down our bus. Before we understood what was going on our driver stopped by the highway-roadside. All cars enroute from Benin, were parked on the same side of the highway with everyone standing outside their vehicles spectating ahead in the direction of travel. I joined the herd. We barely stood ten minutes when suddenly we saw a bunch of persons in the distance running towards our direction. The moment in time reminded me of a scene from a Clint Eastwood cowboy movie.

Seconds passed before I noticed, I was the last man standing. I looked back and all the people and passengers where running fast and furious (Naija style). Half a second later I finally realised I was in a panic situation and I had to do something about it. There were no blue or red pill issues here. All I thought about were my sons Femi, Seyi and Jasmin. I picked my red rucksack marked with the inscriptions "Grand Prix Bern" and took off as fast as I could. Whilst running I was mentally supported by Usain Bolt. As I ran I heard more gunshots, which sounded more like an exchange. I stopped and threw my light body down on the very hot asphalt. I said to myself: I am ready what ever happens should happen now. I think I stayed glued to the ground for sometime. Suddenly I saw people walking back towards the bus.

That's life for you. In Nigeria anything can happen at anytime. Strangely to me, this road trip was my most interesting in Nigeria. It made me totally alive just like when I met "that lady". I think I need more of such moments now. Our "God is Good" driver whose name was "Change" invited us to board. In less than five seconds we were on our way to Lagos. On arrival at the God is Good bus station some slender passenger lady from our bus said prayers, sprinkled good byes. We all then dispersed as if nothing ever happened.

From the bus stop I took a keke to my local favourite spot. So as I asked myself how I could get more of my Fatherhood, more of "that lady" and more of Nigeria I got a phone call from my dad who was in Switzerland at the time, telling me that my mum, who was on treatment in Switzerland, has just been diagnosed with Parkinson's.

At the time, I was sitting at "mama twelve o'clock buka" enjoying a very cold bottle of coke with some party fried rice and chicken.

I was breaking bad. I felt I had reached my breaking point. My current life's picture currently resembles Israel rather than Nigeria at the moment. It now has a couple of fragments more which are:
- How to deal with the emotional impact of my aging parents keeping in mind I live outside Nigeria.
- Single fatherhood responsibilities. Raising a child is the most rewarding thing I have ever experienced. Being a single father of two kids raises many more flags than being a single woman. Should I ignore my fatherhood responsibilities or live with flashbacks of hearing the sons say "I love you daddy" after putting them to bed?

My life remains a war zone, I feel like a soldier abandoned by its X and Y cultural axis. Currently the "wind" is blowing towards

Nigeria. If I live in Nigeria, I won't be able to see my sons often. Hence, my fatherhood role makes no sense.

I sometimes sit and wonder why I returned my gun at the end of my Swiss military service…

© Stefan Asemota

Production and Publishing:
BoD - Books on Demand, Norderstedt

ISBN 978-3-7392-4805-9

© Postface Photo
James Amuta
Jamesamuta.com